Southern England

Edited by Donna Samworth

WHERE WOULD YOU GO?

ABOUT THIS BOOK ...

First published in Great Britain in 2015 by:

Remus House
Coltsfoot Drive
Peterborough
PE2 9BF
Telephone: 01733 890066
Website: www.youngwriters.co.uk

SB ISBN 978-1-78443-813-5

Printed and bound in the UK by BookPrintingUK
Website: www.bookprintinguk.com

WELCOME TO A WORLD OF IMAGINATION!

Dear Reader,

My First Story was designed for Key Stage I children as an introduction to creative writing and to promote an enjoyment of reading and writing from an early age.

The simple, fun storyboards give even the youngest and most reluctant writers the chance to become interested in literacy by giving them a framework within which to shape their ideas. Pupils could also choose to write without the storyboards, allowing older children to let their creativity flow as much as possible, encouraging the use of imagination and descriptive language.

We believe that seeing their work in print will inspire a love of reading and writing and give these young writers the confidence to develop their skills in the future.

There is nothing like the imagination of children, and this is reflected in the creativity and individuality of the stories in this anthology. I hope you'll enjoy reading their first stories as much as we have.

Jenni Bannister

Jenni Bannister
Editorial Manager

CONTENTS

IMAGINE ...

Children were shown an image featuring a magical talking book asking the question, 'Where would you like to go on an adventure?'

The children then imagined their adventures choosing from one of five storyboards, using the pictures and their imagination to complete the tale - and here are the results!

JUNGLE STORY

Storyboard 1

SPACE STORY

Storyboard 2

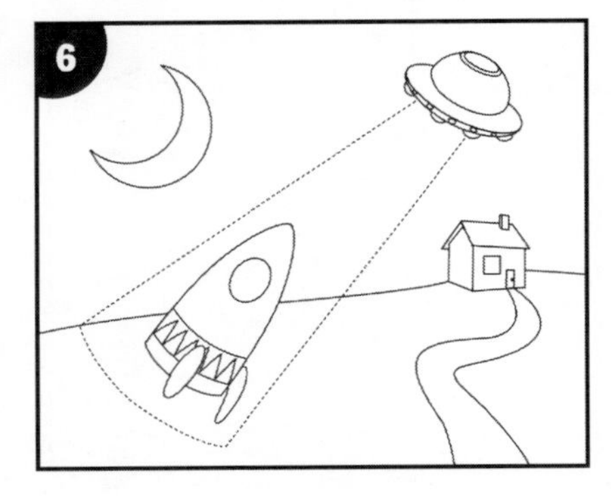

MAGICAL STORY

Storyboard 3

UNDER THE SEA STORY

Storyboard 4

DINOSAUR STORY

Storyboard 5

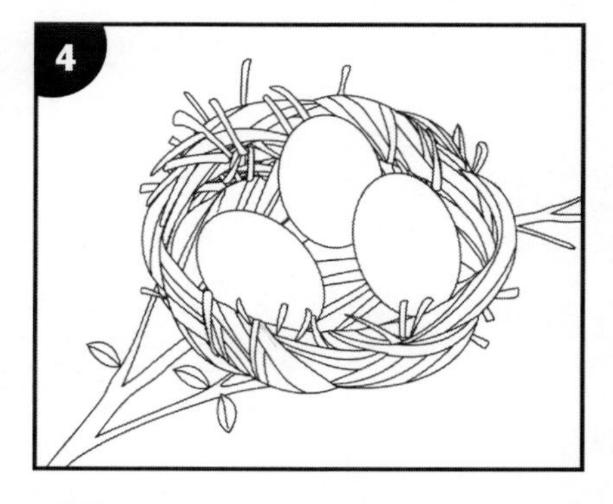

The Stories

Jack's Jungle Story

In the dark, dark woods, in one of the trees, there was a snake. He slid through a branch where you can't see. His colour was green, he was happy. He was quietly listening for something for his tea. But suddenly, the snake found something to eat, so he opened his jaws and it was a lion. Then the snake shut its jaws. The lion was happy. And the lion scared the snake away. But the lion didn't see the snake. The lion ran away in the forest. When he got to the end of the forest, the lion saw a house and a tree next to it so he walked down then he saw even more houses. 'This must be a village,' he said.

Jack Lee

Lucy's Jungle Story

One day, I went to the jungle that was dark and scary. I was walking and suddenly, I heard some hissing in the trees but I did not mind, I just thought it was a bird, but no, it was a snake, a massive snake that was looking to eat me up. Luckily, I could call someone but I forgot my phone. So a tiger came to scare the snake away to a different land, a land far away, in a completely different place. I was scared when the lion came but it seemed like it was friendly but no one else knew that the lion was friendly.

I said to the lion, 'Where do you live?'

The lion said, 'In the cave that is so far away, it will take me ages to get back home to the cave.'

I said, 'I've been past a house and I still know where it is.'

I showed him and he said, 'Thank you.'

Lucy Olivia Jones (6)
Bishop Parker RC Combined School, Milton Keynes

Kathryn's Under The Sea Story

One day, a boat was floating over the sea. It got all dark under the sea because it was the reflection of the boat which was passing. The boat was grey with no one in it.
Under the sea were lots of fish and a crab and there was lots of seaweed. He saw lots of big fish, small fish and different kinds of fish, it was lovely under the sea. Suddenly, a shark came and I swam but the shark was friendly so I invited him for tea. He had popcorn and sweets and lots of other sweetie things, I loved it.
Then a mermaid came and scared him away so I felt sad and I told the mermaid, who was my friend, but she did not listen to me so I cried. Then a merman came and made her cheer and then they invited me for a party. We had cake and sweets. Soon I got tired and full up, I needed a rest.
Then I went to the surface and waved to the boat and said goodbye, I never saw the boat again so I felt sad but I got to meet the shark again.

Kathryn Gibson (7)
Bishop Parker RC Combined School, Milton Keynes

Tiffany's Magical Story

Once upon a time, there was magical place and it was a castle. There was a mean dragon with big wings, scary teeth and no one liked him. One day, it was a happy day and the dragon was very happy because he had a plan to burn the castle down. There was a unicorn and it was kind and nice and pretty.

The dragon breathed fire and he met a pretty unicorn, she said to the mean dragon, 'Hello,' and he said hello back. The pretty unicorn and the mean dragon shook hands. They had a big smile. There was a mean witch and broom, it was very strange. The witch had a green spot on her face and her face was green. She looked very ugly. She had long nails. She had one tooth at the bottom of her mouth. Her hat was long and very, very black.

The day was getting dark, the witch said, 'Come on Broom, I want to go home.' Her house was mad. There was lots and lots and lots of candy.

Tiffany Ama Yeboah Ankamah (6)
Bishop Parker RC Combined School, Milton Keynes

Sophia's Magical Story

Once upon a time, there was a princess called Emily. She lived in a gigantic, pretty castle with flags and there was a green tree.
There was a humongous, big, orange dragon! He had a spiky back, strong bones and sharp teeth. Because of his strong bones, he never lost a fight. It liked to breath mega hot, red, smoky fire that could make metal bend so much that it breaks into two pieces.
Then the orange dragon met a unicorn, it was friendly and white. It liked to play. She became a new friend.
There was a witch with a paintbrush and she made it alive, it was a happy paintbrush and a kind paintbrush. The paintbrush was smiling, it saw a house at night, it was quite dark. There was moonlight so it was not so dark.

Sophia Nganga (7)
Bishop Parker RC Combined School, Milton Keynes

Marcia's Under The Sea Story

One day, Isaac decided to sail the sea in his boat. It was a very small boat for a big boy like Isaac but he could fit in, although he was sixteen. Meanwhile, a crab called Pasty was looking for some fish to eat. He looked very hungry indeed. 'Come out little fish, I'm really hungry,' he said.
Suddenly, Samuel the shark bit a piece of Isaac's boat! Isaac jumped out of the boat and used his necklace to turn into the merman! Pasty hid in his shell. A little mermaid called Amy, saw what happened and called her father, Acrisius. Her father chased Samuel all the way to his mum and never came back. 'If you come back, you will become our slave!' they shouted. Samuel never came back because he didn't like the sound of that!
The mermaids said goodbye to Isaac and swam back to their homes and had lots of fun under the sea.

Marcia Forson (7)
Bishop Parker RC Combined School, Milton Keynes

Kieran's Dinosaur Story

One day, I saw a machine that makes dinosaurs. I sat in the chair and it was very massaging and then I was in the forest. I became a T-rex and there was another T-rex and we both were fighting. Then I won because I bit the T-rex on the back.

I saw a naughty T-rex running away because a daddy T-rex was trying to bite and stomp really hard on him. A flying bird dinosaur laid their eggs in a dinosaur nest. Did you see a dinosaur? Then the dinosaurs ran after the flying dinosaur bird. Then the flying dinosaur flew up into the sky and then landed on a very bright, glittery, beautiful, white cloud in the blue sky.

Then the machine went to the present and I did not have any idea what was going on. Then I read the instructions.

Kieran Gilnagh (7)

Bishop Parker RC Combined School, Milton Keynes

Baqiat's Dinosaur Story

Once upon a time, there was a dinosaur machine. What it did was, you say a dinosaur's name then the dinosaur becomes alive. One day, the small dinosaur saw a dinosaur hunting near a volcano. He was still little so he did not know what to do, so all he did was smile.
Then a huge dinosaur came stomping closer and closer to them. He was vicious at them for playing and hunting where he was because he wanted the place to himself.
Then he saw a nest, the nest was not a dinosaur nest, it was a bird's nest. It looked like a dinosaur's eggs. Suddenly, the three dinosaurs saw how one of the eggs was growling angrily. She was going to her nest. She was a flying dinosaur. She was looking happy.
The machine also asked you if you wanted to be in the past, present or future.

Baqiat Adeogun (7)
Bishop Parker RC Combined School, Milton Keynes

In The Jungle

Once upon a time, there was a spooky jungle. One day a little boy went into the spooky jungle to explore. His mother came looking for him and she went into the jungle as well. A little way in, she met a snake. She thought it was going to bite her but it was a friendly snake, it just wanted to say hello but she just screamed. 'Argh!'
'Don't be scared,' said the snake, 'I won't hurt you'.
Just then, a cobra jumped out of the bush and said, 'I will eat you two.' Then he made a cage by shedding his skin to trap them in. She saw that the cobra had asked his friends to come and see them trapped. Suddenly a big lion parachuted from a tree to the ground using a massive leaf. Then he grabbed onto the cobras' necks and banged their heads together and chucked them in the lake.
Now he had got rid of all the snakes. The lion said he had to go home because he needed to see his grandparents to tell them what happened. Finally, the boy's mum carried on but before she went, she asked if she and her son could come round one day to see the lion's family. He said yes.
She went to look for her son. But he had turned wild.

Santino Palmiero (7)
Bishop Parker RC Combined School, Milton Keynes

Lauren's Under The Sea Story

One day, I went to explore the dark, blue sea. I went in my small, green boat. The waves were calm and slow so I didn't need to worry. Then I saw a beautiful orange crab. It was in a brown, peachy shell. I loved the crab and its shell. The crab smiled at me, I never took my eyes off it but then a big shark came with big, strong teeth. It swam right past the crab but it was coming for me. I didn't know what to do but I decided to pretend that I was dead.
I thought I saw a mermaid. Then I realised I did see a mermaid with a merman, he was holding a trident with triangles on the end. I was so glad they saved me. Everyone was happy, they might have been as happy as me.
I said, 'Thank you for helping me, I can't tell you how happy I am.'
The mermaid and the merman said, 'I am happy that you came.'
I said, 'It's time for me to go now but I'm sure I will see you again.'
They said, 'Yes, we will see you again, all you need is to tell us when you will see us again.'
'Next Tuesday OK?'

Lauren Bell (7)
Bishop Parker RC Combined School, Milton Keynes

Lillie's Under The Sea Story

Once upon a time, there was a boat, the boat was a little small, it was made of wood. There was a friendly crab, some stones, seaweed and fish and starfish. An angry shark swam with sharp teeth and a big lip, it had an angry face on it. It was eating some fish. A bad man came and the shark was still trying to come, then the mermaid and the shark ran away as fast as they could. They all had a big party and the crab was invited and a seahorse came and they were dancing. The boat went home and they stopped having a party and swam up and said, 'We will miss you.'

Lillie Harper (7)
Bishop Parker RC Combined School, Milton Keynes

Bonita's Magical Story

Once upon a time, there was a castle in England. A wonderful queen ruled it. She gave birth to a baby. The dragon of Scotland went to England when the princess was only seven! The dragon ate the queen and the king was dead. The dragon set light to the castle and as for Lily, well she ran away. Lily was the princess you see.
The dragon was finished with the castle. He went on his way and met a unicorn and had a fight with her. A witch found them because she saw the princess and told her broom to save Lily. The broom took Lily to a cosy cottage in the woods.

Bonita Laker (6)
Brook Field Primary School, Swindon

Jacob's Jungle Story

Once upon a time, in a forest, there lived some Emerald Tree Pythons. They were 10 metres long, one of them was only six metres. All the other guys made fun of him, so he left. On his way, he saw a Cobra.
'Hello,' he said, 'I am looking for a friend?'
'I know a good friend for you.'
He is a lion. 'Oh, I like lions.'
'He is smaller than you so be gentle. Bye.'
He finally found him. They slithered and ran to each other. They said 'Hello.' They played all afternoon but then the lion had to go home so they said bye-bye to each other.

Jacob Studholme (6)
Brook Field Primary School, Swindon

Nylah's Under The Sea Story

Once upon a time there lived a small mermaid called Ariel. She lived with her father next to land. Later, she found a person. She told her dad and he said, 'Do not go to see him.'
'Why?'
'Because I said.'
Next she went down to the bottom of the sea but then the big, bad shark came along to chase Ariel. She swam but she got stuck. She cried, 'Help! Help!' Ariel soon was free but the shark was sad. Then she met her dad and he was so proud of her when she had to say goodbye.

Nylah Field (6)
Brook Field Primary School, Swindon

Macy's Space Story

Bob went to the moon and he met aliens. The aliens were taken and he joined in with them. Then he went to his space rocket and he didn't have any petrol so he couldn't move and he met an alien called Bob. One day, Bob the alien asked him, 'Do you want to go inside my spaceship?'

The boy said, 'Yes please.'

'This is the Bob that I have been talking about,' the boy said when he got home.

Macy Pickett (6)

Brook Field Primary School, Swindon

Amelie's Magical Story

Once upon a time, there was a beautiful kingdom and there were lots of people living there. Then a terrible, scary, mean dragon came, it destroyed the whole kingdom. The dragon had really hot fire coming out of his mouth. The dragon was chasing the children, breathing out fire trying to eat them. He was eating the houses.
The dragon came to a magical world where unicorns lived, it was beautiful. The dragon destroyed that world too. A witch had a magic paintbrush, the paintbrush controlled the dragon, the dragon wasn't very nice anyway. The paintbrush went to a house where the dragon lived. It looked like it was an old house, it wasn't very pretty, it was just all black.

Amelie Hunter (6)
Brook Field Primary School, Swindon

Rosie's Under The Sea Story

Once upon a time, there lived a crab, he was called Dylan. He liked swimming so he lived in the sea. Every three days, he went swimming with his friends who were called Freddy and Milly. Also Tilly. He always swam backwards. His friends liked to swim as well. It was his birthday, he was 20, he went under the sea and saw a mermaid fighting with a fish. The fish was getting hurt. Then the mermaid was dancing. Happy, she was dancing with the mermaid king. Then they went out of the water and went home.

Rosie Hawkins (6)

Brook Field Primary School, Swindon

Anthony's Space Story

Once upon a time, there was a spaceship. It was going to go to space. It was called Mars, that was where it was going. Mars is very hot. The spaceship was going to Mars. It was so hot that it was almost burnt by Mars. It was hot. A UFO came and there was an alien in the UFO. It was called Frank.
'Hello,' said Frank. (Frank was the alien who said hello.)
'Hello alien,' said Sam.
The alien was really friendly. The rocket landed on Mars. It was hot that day. The spaceship landed on Mars. They were hot because Mars is hot. When they got home, they were tired and went to bed. At home, the child went to bed.

Anthony Ho (6)
Brook Field Primary School, Swindon

Aashi's Magical Story

Once upon a time, there lived a beautiful princess, her name was Twivelite. Princess Twivelite was magical. One day, a dragon came but it was no matter for the princess because she had magic. The dragon started to breathe fire. The dragon nearly caught the princess. There was a witch who knew the dragon didn't like the unicorn so the witch called her pet unicorn. When the dragon ran away, the witch said well done to her pet unicorn. The unicorn's name was Jessica. Finally, it was time to go home. The witch's wand showed everyone the way home and they lived happily ever after.

Aashi Khaitan (6)
Brook Field Primary School, Swindon

Aadí's Jungle Story

Once upon a time, there lived a snake. It lived in a jungle with tall trees. It lived in a tree with branches on the tree. He was always happy, he coiled up when he was happy. When he was happy, he slept in his tree. After that, he saw a rattlesnake when he passed a bush by his tree. It looked very angry and then he saw a lion. It looked fierce with sharp teeth and claws. Its hair looked scrunched up then they had a battle against each other and the lion ran away because he was scared that he might get killed by the rattlesnake. After that, he saw a house and thought he could have tea and lunch. He knocked on the door. No one was there but the door was already open so he went in and made it his house.

Aadí Nanda (6)
Brookfield Primary School, Sutton

Attia's Magical Story

Once, in a far distant land, there lived a beautiful princess called Angelina. She had long, curly, wavy hair. Just like Rapunzel! She was so pretty, her castle was enormous and pink! But Angelina was not allowed to go outside because there were bad people. There were dragons. Then a dragon flew and he saw the castle. The dragon wanted to come to her lovely castle.

The dragon's skin was a bright orange colour with really sharp, green spikes! His fiery breath came out of his massive mouth. *Roar!* The dragon's name was Steve. When the dragon reached the castle, he met a beautiful unicorn! She was wonderful. The unicorn was friendly and let the dragon be her friend. The unicorn was very pretty and her name was Stella. She had a great, magic horn.

After, when the witch saw that they became friends, she was very angry. But Steve and Stella used Stella's magic and the witch was gone forever. The witch's broomstick escaped and Princess Angelica, Steve, Stella and the broomstick lived happily ever after!

Attia Shanwari (6)

Brookfield Primary School, Sutton

Abigail's Magical Story

Once upon a time there was a princess that never came out of her castle.
One day a dragon came to the castle to destroy it but the princess was OK because the doors were shut. The dragon started to breathe fire so the dragon did.
But the princess's unicorn came to the castle to try and stop the dragon from breathing fire.
A witch made the dragon blow some more fire so she told him to make some more flames. The witch's broomstick wanted to help the princess so he told her to run away from the witch.

Abigail Evans (6)
Brookfield Primary School, Sutton

Hawa's Magical Story

Once upon a time, there was a girl in a big and beautiful castle and her name was Rosie. She was all alone and had no friends. One day, Rosie was standing on the castle balcony looking at the magnificent view, hoping somebody was there to play with her.
Suddenly, she saw a baby dragon flying towards her. Rosie was scared then Baby Dragon said, 'Don't be scared of me because I'm alone and I am finding a friend.'
One day, Rosie and Baby Dragon were playing when a large fireball came out of Baby Dragon's mouth. Rosie was so excited seeing a fireball.
A baby unicorn came running where Rosie and the baby dragon were playing and asked if she could join with them. Baby Dragon said yes and asked, 'What is your name?'
'I am Baby Unicorn, nice to meet you.' They shook hands.
There was a nasty witch, she wanted to have the castle so she sent her broom to spy on the castle. Baby Dragon caught the broom and said, 'I'm going to burn you now.' Broom started to get scared and ran away very scared to his master. They never came back, Rosie, Baby Dragon and Baby Unicorn lived happily ever after in the castle.

HAWA SATAR (6)

BROOKFIELD PRIMARY SCHOOL, SUTTON

Harrison's Dinosaur Story

Once upon a time, I found a time machine. It took me in the past to some dinosaurs. The land was super-duper hot and very noisy. It was full of hungry dinosaurs. I met a T-Rex called Ted who was very friendly. He asked me to help him open a pack of Jaffa cakes as his arms were too tiny to open them.
All of a sudden, me and Ted heard a cracking sound, there were dino eggs hatching. Out popped a pterodactyl baby. The babies' mummy swooped down from the sky to say hello. Her name was Charlotte and she helped to find my time machine. I pressed the button and in a flash, I went home.

Harrison Dalli (5)
Brookfield Primary School, Sutton

Courtney's Under The Sea Story

One sunny day, I went out on my boat. My boat was made of glass so I could see the fish swimming underneath. One of the fish has stripes on it and I saw a crab with sharp claws. I saw a shark and I was scared. My friend Melissa the mermaid, sang and sang so she could scare the shark away. Melissa's dad saved her too. They both lived happily ever after.

Courtney Elizabeth Sculthorpe (6)
Brookfield Primary School, Sutton

Ethan's Dinosaur Story

One day, I went into my garden and I saw a time machine. It looked kind of weird. I jumped on it. The time machine took me to dinosaur land. In dinosaur land, there were lots of dinosaurs. Then I saw a big dinosaur and it found some eggs. So it went to the eggs and he ate the crispy eggs on the tree. And oops, he realised that he was allergic and he sneezed three times. Then I saw the eggs pop out of his mouth. Then I saw a dinosaur with wings.
I went back home and it was very dark because it was night-time so I went to bed.

Ethan Mensah (6)
Brookfield Primary School, Sutton

ABISHAN'S SPACE STORY

Once upon a time, there was a rocket that was flying to space. When it was going to space, it broke its leg. It crashed on a planet. It's leg fell on the planet too. Then a spaceship came and there is an alien in the spaceship. It had five lights. The alien was good and he liked to rescue people. He had three eyes. Then the alien saved the rocket. Then it grabbed the rocket. The spaceship used its magnet power. Finally, the spaceship got the rocket back to its home. It let go of the rocket and they lived happily ever after.

ABISHAN SANJEEVAN (6)
BROOKFIELD PRIMARY SCHOOL, SUTTON

Ben's Dinosaur Story

Once upon a time, there were two boys called Ben and Josh. They wanted to go to Dinosaur Land so they built a time machine. They got into the time machine and they travelled back in time. When they arrived, they heard a mighty roar and it made them look around. When they were walking, Josh said to Ben, 'I think we are being followed by... by... by a T-rex!' The T-rex chased Ben and Josh to the big tree. They clambered up the tree and hid in a pterodactyl's nest. Ben and Josh were so tired so they sat on the eggs for a rest. Then the daddy pterodactyl came home, he was cross and he picked up Ben and Josh and threw them in the time machine. They went home.

Ben Smith (5)
Brookfield Primary School, Sutton

Elsie's Magical Story

Once upon a time there lived a princess called Emily. She had a very pretty castle and she lived in it. One day, a dragon came and it was very sly. It blew the castle down and it had very long claws. The dragon blew fire on the castle and the castle burnt and fell down. Soon, the dragon met a unicorn and they were kind of friends but sometimes have a bad day. One day, a witch came and she had a broomstick that had eyes and the witch was very creepy. The broomstick pointed to a house and the princess lived in it.

Elsie Grace Daley (5)

Brookfield Primary School, Sutton

Evie's Jungle Story

A long time ago, a little boy and girl walked past a jungle and saw small eyes in the wavy trees and bushes. They went into the jungle! Behind the bushes they saw a slimy, green snake that looked friendly. They went to look closer at the snake but it got angry and showed its teeth, then chased them. A friendly lion saw the angry snake chasing the children and decided to help them. The lion ran up to the snake and scared it away by roaring! The lion walked them back to their house and went in for his tea. They all lived happily ever after.

Evie Alice Saunders (6)
Brookfield Primary School, Sutton

Adam's Magical Story

Once upon a time there was a beautiful castle in an amazing land. A fierce dragon, who came from the East, wanted the castle for himself. The dragon was attacking the castle by breathing fire out of his mouth. A good unicorn saw what the bad dragon wanted to do. She decided to help the people in the castle. She asked a witch to trick the dragon with very difficult questions. The dragon couldn't answer them so he had to surrender. He decided to find his own home.

Adam Alves (6)
Brookfield Primary School, Sutton

Giada's Jungle Story

I am Pretsel the honey badger and today, I will tell you about my adventure in the jungle.

The jungle is a very wild and scary land, home to the most dangerous creatures on Earth. It can be a very challenging place, even for a fearless animal like me. On my first day in the jungle, I felt very lonely. I saw a snake slithering on a tree branch, it was long but had a very gentle face and I thought we could be friends.

I approached him and asked for his name, but all of a sudden he turned into the scariest creature I have ever met. Its mouth opened widely, ready to grip his fangs and inject his poison into me. I was petrified but then I found the strength to run away.

As soon as I was safe, I realised that the snake wasn't friendly after all. I caught my breath and kept on walking until I saw a huge, fierce lion, and I thought to remain still and quiet behind the tall plants until the lion had gone away.

All of a sudden, two large paws swept away the leaves I was hiding behind and a huge creature said: 'Cooco!' with a very playful and gentle voice and there it was where I met my dearest friend, Lio the lion.

Together, we spent days exploring the jungle, having the most wonderful time of our lives. In spite of appearance, Lio was a very gentle creature and when it was time for me to get back home, we promised each other that we would always stay friends. My adventure in the jungle has taught me that I should never judge others over their appearance.

Giada Muntoni (7)
Brookfield Primary School, Sutton

Arianne's Magical Story

Once upon a time, there was a little kingdom with a king, queen and a princess inside. But there was an evil dragon in front of the castle who breathed fire. One day, the terrible dragon burned the village, it made the king extremely cross.
The scary dragon met a pretty unicorn with pretty pink hair. But next to the castle was a tall tower with a wicked witch inside the biggest tower, she had a smiling broom. The smiling broom ran away from the witch and lived happily ever after.

Arianne Tucker (6)
Brookfield Primary School, Sutton

Ben's Jungle Story

One cold and shivery night some eyes were spying from the woods. The next day, a snake was slithering on a tree branch and then slipped down to find some food. Something caught his eye in the leaves. He was very surprised. A hairy looking thing popped out of the leaves. It was Lion, Snake's best friend. Then Lion played with Snake all day, they played chase and hide-and-seek. It was so fun. Soon, it was time to go home. 'Bye-bye,' said Lion. Snake said bye-bye back then Lion happily strolled home.

Ben Musters (6)
Brookfield Primary School, Sutton

Beth's Magical Story

Once upon a time, there was a castle and a rainbow. There was a princess and the princess looked out of the window, and there was a dragon who was terrifying and breathing fire and he looked hungry and ferocious. Suddenly, a beautiful unicorn came and another dragon, they shook hands and a witch was spying. She was wicked and she had a broomstick. Then the broomstick put a spell on them.

Beth A M Farmer (5)

Chiseldon Primary School, Swindon

Alicja's Magical Story

Once upon a time, there lived a lonely, beautiful unicorn, she didn't have any friends. One day, the unicorn met an unfriendly dragon, they tried to shake hands but when the unicorn saw a witch casting her spell, the unicorn said, 'Help! Help! There's a witch!'

The dragon breathed out its fire and chased the witch away. Just then, a broomstick appeared and said, 'Excuse me. Where's my master?'

'We do not even know where she is,' replied the dragon with a smile. Just then, a castle appeared. 'Maybe the witch is in the castle,' said the broomstick to himself. Because she was not there, the dragon ate the broomstick. That was the end of the broomstick.

Alicja Pieron (5)
Chiseldon Primary School, Swindon

The Amazing Adventure

One day, Holly and James were playing in the attic and having a great time. Then Holly noticed something wrapped up in a big cloth, she called James, 'Come over here,' she shouted. James came over right away. They pulled the cover off, then there stood a shiny but old time machine.

Holly and James stepped into the time machine. James pulled the levers. First nothing happened, so James pulled it again. Then Holly oiled it and then *poof*, they were in the dinosaur age.

'Hello!' squealed Holly.

'Uh-oh,' whispered James.

Suddenly, they both realised that they were in the dinosaur age. Then a volcano was about to erupt. James and Holly quickly ran to the time machine.

Then the pterodactyl was trying to get the time machine so they ran even faster. James got in there first then Holly got there second. Holly pulled the lever and *poof*, they were back home. Then they got out of the time machine and wrapped it back up again. Then Holly and James never played with the time machine ever again.

Madeleine Clark (7)

Chiseldon Primary School, Swindon

The Adventure Of The Lost Dinosaurs

One day, a girl called Holly and a boy called Harry were playing in the dark wood. Then they wanted some pine cones so they went to get some. Holly was nine so she knew where to look. Harry was five so he would hold Holly's hand.

While they were looking they saw some leaves. They were all piled up on top of each other. So Holly and Harry unpiled them and found a rusty time machine. Holly and Harry decided they would go back in time but where to? Harry wanted to go to the dinosaurs because he loved dinosaurs. So they did.

When they got there, they saw very colourful dinosaurs and started to explore, but then the trees moved, it was a dinosaur. They ran as fast as they could. Then Holly remembered the time machine and where it was. She led the dinosaur to it, they got in and went home and had a cup of tea to calm them down.

Aimeé Bosher (7)

Chiseldon Primary School, Swindon

The Dinosaur Adventure!

Logan and Jeremy were playing in the big attic, they loved playing in the attic because there were lots of old toys and they liked it because they had lots of room to run around in. Logan was zero months old and Jeremy was ten years old. Logan was greedy, Jeremy was funny.
As they were playing, they saw something under a cover so they pulled the cover off and it was a dirty, rusty, old time machine so they went in but the problem was they didn't know where they were going so they screamed for help. Luckily they were in the portal but no help was found.
Suddenly, they were in a completely different place and there were lots of dinosaurs like T-rexes. This was their first ever adventure in their lives but Jeremy was very grumpy because he had to push Logan everywhere. Logan really wanted to explore so they went out to explore and saw lots of amazing things and one of the dinosaurs said, 'Can you stay?'
But Jeremy said, 'No sorry.'
Then Jeremy said, 'I have to go home. I can come another day.'

Harriet Eggett (7)
Chiseldon Primary School, Swindon

The Adventures Of Jack

One day, there was a boy called Jack, he liked Lego, he was six and the youngest in his class. Then to his amazement, a portal appeared, then he jumped through and it took him back in time. Suddenly, he was in dinosaur times.
Suddenly, a T-rex came barging in, luckily he had his pack with him. He found a sword but he didn't know what to do. Then he got really strong and sliced his guts out then he realised the portal came back and he got sucked back.

Jack Telling (6)
Chiseldon Primary School, Swindon

The Dino Adventure

One day, Maddie and Olly were playing in the living room. Mum said,
'Can you move to the attic?'
'OK,' said Olly.
'Let's go,' said Maddie.
They went into the attic, then they started playing dinosaurs. They were using boxes as volcanoes. They found cardboard to make dinosaurs. They found a humongous box, they looked inside and saw a time machine! They teleported into a dinosaur's mouth. Maddie and Olly heaved at the walls.
'It's no use,' said Maddie.
'Wait,' said Olly, 'We can get out.'
'I know what you're thinking,' exclaimed Maddie.
'What then?' said Olly.
'You're going to kill him,' said Maddie.
'No, no, no and no. We'll knock his tooth out!' exclaimed Olly.
Olly plunged towards it and swung then chopped off a tooth. They quickly teleported back to the attic.

Oliver Garner (7)
Chiseldon Primary School, Swindon

The Time Machine

One day, Jane and Mikell were playing in the dusty attic. There were lots of big cobwebs and Jane was very scared of cobwebs but Mikell wasn't scared of cobwebs at all. Jane and Mikell were looking for something to play with in the attic.

Then Jane and Mikell heard a cracking sound, it came from the back of the attic. Jane ran over to see what it was then Mikell ran over to see what it was. Jane and Mikell couldn't believe their eyes, it was a time machine. Jane was desperate to know where it took you.

Then Jane sat on the time machine, she had disappeared. Mikell sat on the time machine then Mikell ended up in a forest. Mikell shouted, 'Jane, Jane, where are you?' and something replied, it was young Jane. Suddenly, the time machine made a sound. 'How are we going to get home?' Then Jane realised the time machine was working so they got on and they ended up back in the attic with a thud. They then went down for tea.

Estella Smith (7)

Chiseldon Primary School, Swindon

The Epic Time Travel!

One day, there was a girl called Daisy and a boy called Joshua, they went to the circus that was very funny but then they saw a time machine and they gasped in amazement. After that, Daisy and Joshua jumped in!
Then they were in dinosaur days. They saw different dinosaurs like a spinosaurus, a pterodactyl, a diplodocus and a stegosaurus. Then a T-rex came barging in and started chasing Daisy and the T-rex caught Daisy and ate her in one gulp. Then Joshua had an idea! He climbed on its head and held onto its ear and started to scream.
Then the dinosaur was sick and Daisy was free and the time machine was back to collect them and they were all safe and sound.

Beatrice Long (7)
Chiseldon Primary School, Swindon

James' Space Story

The rocket zoomed in space and it found black sky. A rocket zoomed very fast, it crashed on Mars. The flying saucer was sparkly and it went past the rocket. An alien found the spaceship and he was kind. The alien picked up the rocket. The alien took the rocket back home.

James Gabriel Ross (6)
Cranmore School, Leatherhead

Jack's Space Story

A silver rocket shot out of the moon. A zooming rocket came with a broken engine and crashed on a planet called Mars. A saucer was zooming round the moon and the saucer saw the spaceship. An alien was a kind alien. The alien helped them. The spaceship helped them. They went back into space. Then they went home and they were friends forever.

Jack Dorricott (6)
Cranmore School, Leatherhead

Lorenzo's Space Story

A shiny, silver rocket zoomed from the Earth. *Crash! Kaboom! Wallop!* Just then somebody realised that they were somewhere near the moon. A flying spaceship came down. 'Argh!' In the spaceship, they were afraid. An alien waved at them, it was a friendly alien. He waved back, the alien was so kind. He picked up the spaceship. They said thank you and waved. The alien took them home. They were almost home, they were hungry!

Lorenzo Mascolo (6)

Cranmore School, Leatherhead

Tommy's Space Story

A rocket came from the black sky.
Bang! It crashed on the moon.
A green flying saucer was hovering above the spaceship.
An alien was in the spaceship and it had three eyes, it was happy.
The alien lifted it up into the sky.
It was heavy. It went into space.

Tommy Williams (5)
Cranmore School, Leatherhead

Jerome's Space Story

The silver rocket zoomed past the clouds, it was out of control. It crashed on a big red planet called Jupiter. A window broke off. A big, green, sparkly flying saucer was hovering around the crash. An alien came out of the spaceship, he had three eyes and he was green and shiny and friendly. The spaceship was picked up by the friendly alien. He took him home. He said, 'Home sweet home.'

Jerome Simon Barnes (6)

Cranmore School, Leatherhead

Alexander's Space Story

There was once a spacecraft that was launched from the USA. But something went wrong with one of the jets. Suddenly, something went *bang!* Then their craft crashed into the moon! Just then, out of nowhere, there came a flying saucer. It appeared with a green, fluffy alien inside. He popped inside their spacecraft and sucked them up and carried them off. They travelled days and nights. The spacemen were bored of travelling around in space all the time. They went over fields and over mountains until they got home.

Alexander Hayward (5)

Cranmore School, Leatherhead

Zac's Space Story

One day, a space rocket crash-landed on the moon, it landed in a puff of smoke. There was an alien that came to help him. Suddenly, a flying saucer came from nowhere and helped. He was friendly. 'I will help you.' So he took him home in his flying saucer. When he got home, it was dark and the alien tucked him in.

Zac Sherazee (6)
Cranmore School, Leatherhead

Gabriel's Space Story

One day, an alien spacecraft flew to Mars but the engine broke so he crashed on the moon. He stayed there for nine years and only had three fish finger sandwiches and had nine gold chocolate bars. On the 10th year, he saw a shiny alien spacecraft coming to where he crashed on the moon. A funny looking alien came. He was a legendary alien, he came to help. The alien that crashed climbed into his alien spacecraft and was lifted up. The legendary alien took the crashed alien home.

Gabriel Asher Ladds (6)
Cranmore School, Leatherhead

Gerry's Space Story

There was once a rocket who wanted to go to Mars, but he got stuck in space. The rocket broke its wing and he crashed on the moon. Suddenly, out of nowhere, a flying saucer came. The alien named Glob was slimy and gooey and green. His flying saucer hovered over the rocket and sucked it up. The flying saucer took it home.

Geronimo Devitt (6)
Cranmore School, Leatherhead

Austin's Space Story

Out of nowhere, a rocket came. It was so fast the engine broke down. It crashed on the cheesy moon. It was stuck. A flying silver, shiny saucer came zooming to land on the moon. A green, happy alien popped out. 'I'll help,' said the alien. He beamed the shiny rocket up with her beeper. The astronaut didn't know what was happening. The alien took the rocket home and fixed it.

Austin Alan Barnes (6)
Cranmore School, Leatherhead

Brendan's Space Story

The UK blasts off a rocket - going to Mars. An engine broke. The rocket crashed on Jupiter. They were far from home, they were there for days on end with no food or water. On the 100th day, a shiny, red flying saucer came. It was Harry their alien friend they met all those years ago.

'Do you need a lift?'

'Yes!' they said.

'OK,' said Harry and he pressed a button and they got lifted up and all the way home. Harry even opened the door for them.

Brendan Clarke (6)

Cranmore School, Leatherhead

Edward's Space Story

One day in space, there was a space rocket. Then an annoying sound was getting louder. It was broken. It crashed on the moon. The spacemen came out with the tools but they could not fix it. Then an alien came to help, his name was Bob, it landed on Mars, it was super. Bob lived there, he was just going to open his door when some strange men tapped Bob on the shoulder. He turned around.
He said, 'Is your space rocket damaged?'
'Yes it is,' said the spacemen.
He hopped in his ship, so did the spacemen.
'I will take you home.'
'Thank you.'
What will happen next?

Edward Richard Agar (6)
Cranmore School, Leatherhead

Tomeka's Dinosaur Story

I went on a time machine to a far away land.
When I got there I saw lots of dinosaurs. There were all different kinds and some had very sharp teeth and claws.
The sharp teeth was for eating meat.
There were dinosaur eggs in a nest which will hatch soon.
I saw a pterodactyl flying up over the clouds, then it came down almost on my head.
I was very scared and ran back to the time machine to take me safely home.

Tomeka Thomas (5)
Good Shepherd RC Primary School, Croydon

Salem's Jungle Story

Last week, Denicia and I decided to go by car to the jungle for a visit. When we got there, we discovered a very large and beautiful space, with big and incredible sized trees, we'd ever seen in our lives. We started walking, taking photos and using our binoculars to admire the beautiful place.
Then we discovered a very large and scary snake laying on a tree. As we approached the tree where it laid, we decided to film with our camera.
Suddenly, the scary and angry snake tried to bite us. We were afraid and started to run fast and faster.
Unfortunately for us, a ferocious and angry lion heard some noises and decided to have a look. Once he saw us running, he started running behind us.
It was a large, strong-flesh animal chasing in order to catch and gobble us. We continued to run, run and found a house with a door open. We entered and closed the door behind us.
The lion stopped running and could not believe how he missed this opportunity to gobble us.

Salem Mutshipayi (7)
Good Shepherd RC Primary School, Croydon

Aaron's Jungle Story

One day in a scary jungle were all kinds of animals live, I came across a small, slimy snake, who was hiding in a big, big tree.
A little boy called Ben, his mum and dad, walked past the tree where the snake was. They did not know he was watching them.
All of a sudden, the snake slid off the tree. He wanted to trip them over but a friendly lion came and grabbed the snake with his big mouth and threw him into the air.
The lion did some tricks for Ben and his mum and dad and they all lived happily ever.

Aaron Richardson (6)

Good Shepherd RC Primary School, Croydon

Daniel's Jungle Story

I went to the zoo in the middle of the forest, it was quite dark and scary, however, the sun was shining through. This was actually very exciting!
I saw different animals from a distance, for example; lion, snakes, monkeys, chimpanzees and giraffes. I was so frightened, but my mum reassured me.
I saw a snake wiggling its tongue. I quickly took a picture of it. It's eyes were so scary and amazing.
I saw a baby lion playing with her mum. It was tiny and so cute. I took its picture too. It looked at me straight in the eyes.
The lions were running up and down the zoo. They were enjoying themselves. I asked for permission to throw the ball at them, and this was granted.
Soon it was time for us to leave the zoo. I saved all my photos for future purposes. What an adventure.

Daniel Okeke (5)
Good Shepherd RC Primary School, Croydon

Taelor's Jungle Story

One day Ella went to a jungle to explore with her friend, Bexs. They took camping gear, flashlights and food. Bexs was scared of the dark and started to quiver when she saw glowing eyes staring back at her. The next morning, there was a snake in the tree above their heads. The girls screamed and ran.

The snake awoke, lifted its head and hissed, showing its fangs. Ella and Bexs stopped running and saw a lion cub that appeared to be smiling at them. The lion cub was friendly and wanted to play. Ella and Bexs played fetch with the lion, who they named Furry.

They knew that they could not take Furry home but every year, when they go camping, they go to the same spot and find Furry with his mum.

Taelor Prendergast (7)
Good Shepherd RC Primary School, Croydon

Denicia's Jungle Story

I am going on an adventure into the woods because I am Super Girl and I am very brave.
I won't be scared of any snakes or any creatures because I'm brave and I am Super Girl.
I saw a scary cobra snake but he did not scare me because I used my super powers and he ran away.
I met a very lovely lion and we played with each other and we defeated all the mad creatures.
The lion took me all around the woods and showed me the lovely places around the woods. We had lots of fun.
When it was morning, it was time to go home, so the lion showed me the way home.

Denicia Tomlin (7)
Good Shepherd RC Primary School, Croydon

Saphir's Dinosaur Story

Salem and I decided to go by car to the land of dinosaurs for a visit last week.
When we got there, we saw a beautiful land with incredible dinosaurs of all sizes, such as; stegasaurus, brachiosaurus. They were walking in this marvellous space with trees. We were so far, we made a decision to use our binoculars to watch them.
As we were looking at them, one of the dinosaurs felt our presence, pointing his eye forward and shouting. We were afraid and decided to run away.
On our way, we saw a nest with three white, big eggs. We had never seen anything like it in our lives. We took some pictures and then, from a distance, we saw another dinosaur flying towards us in the sky.
We finally decided to stop our adventure and return home by car. Maybe we will go back there next month.

Saphir Mutshipayi (4)
Good Shepherd RC Primary School, Croydon

Lifejoy's Dinosaur Story

The magic chair takes me to the past, present and future. I want to go to the past to see the dinosaurs.
I have landed in the dinosaur land. I can see a stegosarus and brachiosaurus.
The tyrannosaurus rex is hiding to catch its prey.
I can see three huge dinosaur eggs in a nest sitting on a branch of a tree.
I can see a pterodactyl flying above the clouds.
The magic chair is taking me back to the present, so I can go back home from my wonderful dinosaurs.

Lifejoy St Basilwudike (5)
Good Shepherd RC Primary School, Croydon

Daniel's Jungle Story

I went on an adventure in Africa. I went to a forest. It was green and scary.
The snake was called Chanei.
Another snake was called David. He lived in a cave. It was dark.
A lion came to save me. He took me to the woods. I saw a friend.
The lion left me. He didn't eat me up!
He took me home. I saw my mum.

Daniel Quartey (5)

Good Shepherd RC Primary School, Croydon

Elaine's Jungle Story

Once upon a time, in a very dark, scary, creepy woods, there was a very, very sharp toothed and clawed monster. 'Roar!' he said.
The monster saw a snake, he looked as cute as a butterfly.
Then the monster took him to marry him.
As soon as he touched it, it turned into a gigantic snake.The monster said, 'Run! Run! Run!'
Then he put it back down and it was a cute tiger.
One day he found a friend.
The next day he found a home to live in.

Elaine Mary Frimpong (5)
Good Shepherd RC Primary School, Croydon

Leona's Dinosaur Story

Once upon a time I sat on a time machine.
It sent me back to where dinosaurs were first brought up.
I saw one of the most dangerous animals called a T-rex.
I then found dinosaur eggs from a dinosaur that can fly.
Then I found the time machine and then went back home.

Leona Freitas (4)
Good Shepherd RC Primary School, Croydon

Kosisochi's Dinosaur Story

One day I went to my garden and I saw a time machine. The machine took me to see dinosaurs. I was scared and lonely.
Some dinosaurs ate plants and some ate meat. They were not nice dinosaurs. I was trying to find my mum and dad.
I ran away from the dinosaurs to find a place to hide, but I saw a tyrannosaurus running to me and it was saying, 'Roar!'
There were three eggs in the nest, but I had to stay there until the T-rex was gone. Then the eggs broke and there were small dinos.
Then big dinosaurs came and took me out of the nest! We were flying for a long time. When it dropped me, I saw the time machine.
I went back home. I was very happy and I went in the house to see my family and I played with them.

Kosisochi Asadu (5)
Good Shepherd RC Primary School, Croydon

Augusta's Jungle Story

In a green, dark, bushy rainforest, lots of trees were growing and hedges were around the edge of the rainforest. Someone came and chopped them down.
Then a slithery snake came up on a tree looking for food to eat. He was going to look on the ground because he was hungry and looking mischievous.
Then came the most scariest creature of the rainforest. A poor baby lion was hiding in the bush because he was scared and he was shivering. Then the baby lion popped out with a joyful face and looking so cute. He had sharp claws and fluffy fur and it was combed nicely.
The little baby lion started to chase something because it was hungry. Its bushy tail flapped around its body and it had an awkward smile. After the baby lion found a cottage and standing up. He has tiny ears and there was a tree near the cottage and there were four hedges.

Augusta Stevens (6)
Good Shepherd RC Primary School, Croydon

Nerea's Magical Story

It was a beautiful sunny day in the Kingdom of Destiny, suddenly drifting over, some dark clouds appeared, it started to rain, a colourful rainbow was formed. Floating just below the rainbow was the sparkling jewel of destiny. Guarding the precious jewel was a small, red, ferocious dragon, swooping around the jewel, with his long, feisty wings. He wasn't alone, he had a friend...
If anyone came close to the jewel, the dragon would grow angry and become bigger and bigger until fire exploded out of his mouth! Before sunset each day, the dragon played with his friend the unicorn, this would be an ideal time to steal the jewel.
The wicked witch that lived nearby had been spying on the dragon and the unicorn, this is how she knew this would be the perfect time to steal the jewel. Knowing this, she saw the opportunity and quickly soared up in the air, and swooped down and grabbed the jewel, making her invisible.

Nerea Kries-Margaroli (7)
Lancing College Prep At Worthing, Worthing

Louie's Magical Story

Once there was a beautiful castle on a hillside and a rainbow above the castle. But one day, a big, red, scaly dragon attacked the castle. Suddenly, he blew fire all over the castle. He blew the castle to smithereens. But a bright unicorn came, then they had a big fight. Suddenly, an ugly witch came and scared everyone away. Everyone ran as fast as they could. However, the witch fell off her broom and was never seen again.

Louie Peter Readman-Berry (7)
Lancing College Prep at Worthing, Worthing

Emma's Magical Story

In a massive castle, on a big, lovely hillside, surrounded by green trees, you could often hear a tremendous roaring noise. One day, the local villagers from down the hill saw what was making the tremendous roar. it was a mighty dragon which was small, but fierce. The next day, the dragon had grown bigger in one night, how amazing! Then the dragon started to burn down some large trees with his flaming fire. Suddenly, the dragon saw a beautiful unicorn with sparkling eyes.
'Don't burn down the wood', said the unicorn, 'my friend Brian the broomstick is wood'.
'I'm so sorry, I was having fun, but I would love to see your friend Brian.'
Just then, the kind witch came over the beautiful hill.
'Did I hear someone call my name?' said Brian the broomstick.
'Yes', said the unicorn, 'There is a nice dragon who wants to meet you'.
'That sounds exciting', said Brian the broomstick, 'Let's all go back to my house, I have some freshly baked apple pie and tea that we can all share.'

Emma Saunders (7)
Lancing College Prep At Worthing, Worthing

Dominic's Magical Story

One day, in a beautiful kingdom, there lived a handsome prince. But the problem was a horrible, vicious dragon came every dark, full moon night. All it did was breathe fire at houses all night long. The full moon came. 'Get in,' said the prince's friend, Jesus. But when he saw that, the dragon came because the dragon heard it. So the dragon flew to the kingdom.

When the dragon got to the kingdom, he tried to get the tall tower down by breathing fire on it. The villagers were all terrified. They ran away and left the prince and his friend, Jesus.

Meanwhile, a pretty princess was at the shop, Asda. You know the one I mean? She was buying some of those weird Asda's own chocolate and some original Pringles to take back for the prince and Jesus' supper. But little does she know, Jesus and the prince were getting attacked by a dragon in the kingdom.

Next, what does the dragon do? I reckon he goes for something else. I mean another part of the castle. Oh, I was wrong. A wand goes to a house. I think the fight stopped. I'll go and check. Yes, it's stopped. It ended up good, the prince won by throwing his sword at the dragon.

Dominic Frost (8)
Lancing College Prep At Worthing, Worthing

Sophie's Under The Sea Story

There was once a boat on the water. It was fishy because it had fish in it. It stank because it was very old. It was old and dirty, brown and smelly. Yuck! It was now empty. There was a crab on the boat, the boat twirled upside down. The fish were glad, scaly and thin. The water was crystal clear and shining. The seaweed was green and slimy. Yuck!
The shark was tempted to make the mermaid jump! 'Yelp!' said the shark, he had hurt himself and the mermaid heard the shark. 'Boo!' shouted the shark! The mermaid did not panic. The mermaid panicked the shark. The shark was more cold-blooded because sharks are cold-blooded. The mermaid was looking yummy! The mermaid scared the shark, the shark ran.
The mermaid looked satisfied. 'Yes, now I can go out in the sea by myself,' and they celebrated.
'Yes,' said the mermaid.
'Let's party,' exclaimed the king.
'Bye crab,' said the king and the mermaid, 'Thank you for all your help.'
'Bye, see you soon.'
'Bye,' said the mermaid and the king.
'Good luck.'

Sophie Went (7)
Lancing College Prep At Worthing, Worthing

Theo's Jungle Story

In the forest, there was a snake.
It was kind.
The snake was going through the jungle bushes.
The tiger came out the bush, it had got red fur.
The tiger was running home.

Theo Anthony Robert Wilkinson (6)
Lovelace Primary School, Chessington

Harmonie's Under The Sea Story

Once upon a time there lived a crab. He lived in the Pacific Ocean (it was very hot). He dreamed to be a hero but every time he tried to save other creatures everything would go wrong.
One day Crab was walking along the ocean, immediately Crab turned round and saw a big huge shark chasing two mermaids. Crab ran and hid under some coral.
The next day, Crab saw the big huge shark again, chasing the mermaids and so he had to make the right choice as he wanted to save the mermaids.
Crab got up and chased the shark. However Shark was not scared, he laughed at Crab. Crab was angry. Crab got up again and this time he pinched Shark on his bottom!
The mermaids were delighted and they all had a party. They danced for joy. 'Whoo! Yippee! We're free!' they said.
Crab said goodbye to the mermaids and Crab became the ocean's greatest hero.

Harmonie Sall (7)
St Elizabeth's Catholic Primary School, Richmond

Molly's Jungle Story

Once there was a little boy called Albert, he had just moved into a new house. Albert saw a magical door that was telling him to go inside so he did. When he went in he saw this amazing place, it took Albert about ten minutes to know where he was. 'I'm in the jungle!'
He saw some bats and snakes hanging off trees. Then he saw a vicious cobra that tried to take him. Suddenly a lovely lion said, 'Go away or I will give you kisses!' So he chased the cobra all the way to his home. Albert could now go home.

Molly Andrews (7)
St Elizabeth's Catholic Primary School, Richmond

Isabelle's Under The Sea Story

It was a peaceful day off the coast of Sydney, Australia. An abandoned boat was floating on the surface of the Pacific Ocean. On the seabed, the sealife of Seaweed Valley were gossiping about what the strange object floating above them was!
'I heard it was a new predator!' exclaimed Crab.
'A new predator?' interrupted Shark. 'I'm number one predator around here!'
Before Shark could even finish his sentence, all of Seaweed Valley had scurried into their shells. 'I'm going to destroy this predator!' announced Shark.
'No you are not!' a voice shouted from the distance. 'Back off you silly shark!' A pair of merpeople came into sight and chased the shark.
The merpeople swam down to Seaweed Valley to reassure the creatures that there was nothing to worry about. 'It's not a predator, it's just our boat,' explained the merman.
The mermaid went on, 'In fact we are half-human and when we are out of water our tails become legs!'

The merpeople swam up to get back on their boat to carry on their adventures on land (with legs).

ISABELLE HAMMOND (6)
ST ELIZABETH'S CATHOLIC PRIMARY SCHOOL, RICHMOND

Joseph's Space Story

I am invited to a party in space by aliens. They told me not to be late.
So I'm working on a rocket to get there.
There will be yummy food and tasty treats. They will fill up my tummy and make me dance because they are yummy.
Different spaceships will come to the party. My rocket will be different colours and powered by fire fuel.
When I arrive there are musical instruments, We play fun games like jump to planets and alien tag.
When we play jump to planets I crash my rocket. I have to be rescued by the alien spaceship.
After the party a friendly alien takes me and my rocket home. All the aliens have a party at my house.

Joseph Goodyer (6)
St Joseph's Catholic Primary School, Haywards Heath

Oscar's Dinosaur Story

Long, long ago lived a man with crazy wild hair. One day the time machine went *flash!* when the man was sitting on it.
Suddenly he was in a mysterious place where giant spotty and spiky creatures roamed the volcano and trees filled the land. 'What am I doing here?' he said.
The man explored this new and unknown world, while searching for useful things a velociraptor was scavenging for prey.
The fearsome velociraptor and the brave time traveller were both looking for food as their tummy rumbled like thunder. Both man and beast spied the eggs in a nest.
The eggs looked so delicious they didn't see each other walking towards the nest until *bang!* They bumped heads. Before the man could get eaten, the mummy pterodactyl swooped down and distracted the velociraptor, while the man had time he flew onto his time machine and he flicked the switch to 'present' and flew safely home.

Oscar Martin (7)
St Joseph's Catholic Primary School, Haywards Heath

Hannah's Magical Story

Once upon a time there was a beautiful princess. Her name was Bella and she lived in a magnificent magical castle.
Bella's castle was very cold. But luckily nearby there was a red fire-breathing dragon so she thought she would ask him to heat her castle up.
The dragon wanted to help so he soared up into the sky and *whoosh!* in a flash he breathed out his fiery breath and lit up the sky, heating the castle from above.
As the dragon came back to Earth he met a petrified, pink unicorn. She told him that Princess Bella had been captured by a wicked witch. Suddenly the wicked witch spotted them both and flew off on her broomstick, taking Bella to her sweetie cottage. The unicorn and the dragon raced after her.
The kind broomstick showed the dragon to a secret door. The dragon burnt the door down and rescued Bella. Before the witch could cast an evil spell on them, Bella, the dragon, unicorn and broomstick all flew back home to the castle.

Hannah Crofts (7)
St Joseph's Catholic Primary School, Haywards Heath

Louis' Jungle Story

There was a jungle called Dark Wood. In the jungle there was a snake, a lion and a giant boa constrictor. It can be very dark and scary sometimes.
The snake can slither around your neck like a worm and it can bite you with its razor-sharp teeth that can almost bite through anything.
The boa constrictor isn't very nice, it can swallow you whole after squeezing you, if you came out you would be dead!
The lion was very cheeky and nice and very kind. He was brave and funny. The lion was very good at scaring you.
He always started to chase you when you said hello and he was very fast. He was very, very, very soft like a teddy bear.
I love going to the lion's house for tea because it's nice, small, clean and very, very, very comfortable for sleeping in!

Louis Philpott (7)
St Joseph's Catholic Primary School, Haywards Heath

Rosie's Under The Sea Story

One day two divers went swimming. They went on a small boat into the deep, dark sea. The two divers' names were Mark and Sam. They heard about the magic seashell by their grandads.
Mark and Sam were desperate to see if the magical seashell was real. After they would steal it, but they needed to make a plan. Bob the crab was guarding the magical seashell.
Then came along Hook Fang, the shark. He heard two divers, Sam and Mark. Hook Fang heard the plan. He quickly swam to the merking and mermaid and told them.
The mermaid and the merking shouted, 'Go and fetch all of the fierce sea creatures!' So Hook Fang fetched all of the sea creatures. He told them to go and help Bob the crab.
Mark and Sam found the magical seashell. Suddenly they saw all of the sea creatures swimming up to them. But they felt brave and what they did was they had a fight.
They started to get annoyed at the sea animals so they tiredly swam back to their boat and floated back. The divers were tired and the sea animals lived happily ever after.

Rosie Sambell (7)
St Joseph's Catholic Primary School, Haywards Heath

Holly's Magical Story

One day there was a beautiful pink castle. On top of it it had a coloured rainbow and inside the beautiful castle there was a mean red dragon. The dragon's teeth were as sharp as a knife and its claws were as sharp as its small teeth.
One day the dragon blew some hot sparkly fire from its tiny mouth. Its fire was as hot as the big sun.
After that the dragon met a pink unicorn. They shook their little hands and they liked each other.
One day an evil witch came. She wanted to put a wicked spell on them but the dragon and unicorn were hiding in the castle.
Then it got dark and the broomstick with blue eyes showed the witch where to go.

Holly Phillips (6)
St Joseph's Catholic Primary School, Haywards Heath

Harvey's Space Story

Once a boy called Jack wanted to be a spaceman, so one day Jack made a spacesuit.
He got a rocket and painted it like a rainbow. He went zooming as quickly as a cheetah to space.
He landed on the moon safely. Suddenly Jack saw a UFO whizzing around space.
There standing in the ship was an alien. The alien was waving at Jack.
The alien smiled at Jack.
The alien sucked Jack's spaceship with Jack inside. Jack quickly jumped out of his ship.
Jack met the alien. The alien smiled at Jack and Jack smiled at the alien. They became best friends.

Harvey Boniface (7)
St Joseph's Catholic Primary School, Haywards Heath

Abhinav's Dinosaur Story

On Sunday morning I went to the dinosaur museum. The clock in the museum took me to the land of dinosaurs. T-rex, the king of the dinosaurs, greeted me and took me for a dinosaur adventure.
I met all his friends. Stegosaurus was awesome to watch with a spiky tail. I enjoyed looking at the dinosaur footprint and eggs. I met the longest dinosaur, the brachiosaurus.
I climbed up its long neck and saw the forest. Then I went to the T-rex's birthday party, we had a cheese sandwich, marshmallows, crisps and chocolate cake. We had lots of fun.
The clock took me back to the dinosaur museum. I had lots to share with my family about my dinosaur adventure.

Abhinav Raman (7)
St Joseph's Catholic Primary School, Haywards Heath

Matthew's Dinosaur Story

We were going to go back in time to the Stone Age. We have been inventing a time machine.
We had to press a red button and the lever and it went to the past.
We had arrived. 'Oh no! I see a T-rex around the bush!'
We needed to defend against the T-rex. I saw the T-rex's nest. We stole the eggs so the T-rex got his friend to fight.
His friend had arrived. He was a dinosaur with big spikes.
'Quick, let's get back home before the dinosaurs get us!' and we were back.

Matthew Sheridan (6)
St Joseph's Catholic Primary School, Haywards Heath

Noah's Dinosaur Story

Hi, I am Noah, I have a present that makes me go to the past.
The present is a time machine. I get in it. I am going back to the dino times.
I find a T-rex. I carefully go in its mouth and pull a tooth out so I can study it.
I climb up a big tree, I see a nest with three eggs in. Just then I see their mother, she heads straight towards me.
I swung and land on her back. She drops me back to the time machine.
I go in it. I turn into a human again. The machine brings me home.
'Phew, what an adventure!'

Noah Philpott (7)
St Joseph's Catholic Primary School, Haywards Heath

Emma's Space Story

Me and Holly found a rocket flying in the sky. It was a fabulous rocket flying in the air. The rocket had instructions on how to use it.
The instructions were a great help because we got there in the end. They told us which button to press.
In the rocket we saw all different kinds of planets. Some of the planets were pretty beautiful and colourful.
When we landed on the moon we found an alien. The alien was green and it had three googly eyes.
There was a bright light which was a planet which was showing the rocket to whatever place it wanted to get to.
The planet led the rocket to our house. We knew who was in the rocket because they had a machine. We were happy to be home.

Emma Rochford (7)
St Joseph's Catholic Primary School, Haywards Heath

Joshua's Dinosaur Story

Once upon a time I invented a time machine so I could go and see dinosaurs a long time ago.
When I got there I saw some huge dinosaurs and a gigantic volcano.
Then out of the leaves came a T-rex and it had very sharp teeth.
The T-rex was trying to eat the pterodactyl's eggs.
The eggs got eaten by the T-rex.
Then I went back home.

Joshua Finn (6)
St Joseph's Catholic Primary School, Haywards Heath

Reily's Space Story

It is lovely and warm on Spicy Planet. Bob the alien is lost and needs help.
Very far away on Jupiter, Reily the alien explorer hears Bob calling for help.
Reily decides to rescue Bob. He gets in his green spaceship and quickly flies to Spicy Planet.
So, back on Spicy Planet Bob is feeling sad because he thinks no one is coming to help. Bob's spaceship is broken.
Then Reily comes back to Planet Spicy and he finds Bob in the Black Forest. Bob is very happy.
Then Reily takes him back to his home. When they get there Bob's mum and dad are so happy and Reily stays for fish and chips.

Reily Driscoll (6)
Seaford Primary School, Seaford

RIDA'S SPACE STORY

Once, there was a good alien called Julius and a bad alien named Meana. Julius lived on Saturn and Meana lived on the moon.
One day Julius didn't have any water so he planned on going to Earth to get water, but Meana didn't have any water and she wanted the water all for herself!
So she made a trap with a net on top of Earth so that Julius couldn't go to Earth. Meanwhile Meana would float to the other side of Earth and get water from there!
'Oh no!' sobbed Julius.
But Julius saw Meana's plan and he had Earth friends, so with his phone he called the mayor and got somebody to throw the net away into space.
Then Julius hopped on his spaceship and he went down to Earth before Meana. Julius decided to stay at Earth to have fresh water for ever and ever.
You may remember Meana, what happened to her? Well she was being chased by a huge mighty red asteroid! 'Noooo!' loudly cried Meana.

Rida Muhamed Rasalie (7)
Seaford Primary School, Seaford

Rory's Magical Story

Once upon a time there was a dragon who lived in a castle.
One day a wicked witch came to the castle and the dragon and the witch had a fight.
The ugly witch was soon dead.

Rory Beaumont (6)
Seaford Primary School, Seaford

Ryan's Space Story

One day there was a good alien on Mars called Good DJ1. He wanted to go to Earth and live on Earth but a bad alien called Bad DJ2 appeared. Bad DJ2 said, 'I won't let you live,' and stopped him going to Earth. Good DJ1 was trying and trying but he couldn't do it.
Good DJ1 called the police and Good DJ1 said, 'Help, police, he's trying to stop me from going to Earth!'
Then the police came and Bad DJ2 was scared of the police. The police took him to jail on Earth and Good DJ1 went to Earth.
However, humans were scared of the alien so the police took Good DJ1 to jail.
Then the police went away so Good DJ1 escaped and he helped Bad DJ2 to escape too. They were now friends and went back to the moon!

Ryan Liu (7)

Seaford Primary School, Seaford

Cassidy's Jungle Story

A dragon was out hunting in the forest when suddenly, in the distance he spotted a pack of hunters. They shouted, 'Surrender or you die!'
He stopped in surprise. Mr Bear saw it and killed the hunters and both of them used teamwork to kill the soldiers that came one by one, then more troops appeared.
They were trying to invade all of the planets. It took 5,000 hours to defeat all of them.
The dragon and the bear were fighting and fighting against the troops and they finally won.

Cassidy Mabey (6)
Seaford Primary School, Seaford

JONNY'S JUNGLE STORY

There once was an elephant called John, he was looking for a friend but he couldn't find one.
One day John found a friend but the monkey, Jonathan, didn't want to be John's friend and John wandered onwards.
Then the next day he found another friend, a grass snake, the grass snake was called Mr Cool.
He didn't want to be his friend.
John was tired of trying to find a friend. He wanted to give up until he turned and found a crocodile called Leo. John asked him, 'Do you want to be my friend?'
'Yes!' shouted Leo.

JONNY BARNES-GALLOWAY (6)
SEAFORD PRIMARY SCHOOL, SEAFORD

Samuel's Space Story

One day there lived a good alien called Good DJ2 and there lived a bad alien called Zog and he was trying to destroy Good DJ2 and take over his planet.
But everyone tried to catch him then came a police alien.
The police alien tried to arrest the bad alien who was trying to take over Zog's planet.
When the police alien caught the bad alien Zog, the police alien took the bad alien Zog to Earth but the humans were scared of the bad alien Zog, so the humans ran far, far away from the bad alien.
Zog tried to find the humans and the police said, 'Argh!' The good alien, DJ2 came to destroy Bob.

Samuel Sutters (7)
Seaford Primary School, Seaford

Eloise's Magical Story

Once upon a time there lived a wizard, a princess, a king and a queen.
One day the wizard appeared and bellowed to the princess, 'I'm going to take you away!'
The wizard took the princess to a hidden tower and said, 'I will give you one chance to escape, if not you will have to clean my grubby old roof and chimney.'
She was lucky so she got out and went back to the castle.

Eloise Burns (7)
Seaford Primary School, Seaford

Isabella's Magical Story

Once there was a beautiful princess named Lacey. She had one horse named Matilda and it was a magnificent horse. Then there was a mean and nasty, bad man. His name was Robbie.
One day he saw the beautiful Lacey. He locked her in jail. He was a really bad man.
Then there was a naughty little fight between the man and even the princess and the horse. Then they sorted the fight out and were all friends again.
Then the horse met loads of lovely friends and they were a dragon and a unicorn. They were named Paws and Pepper, they were friends as well.
Then there was a bad thing because then the unicorn and the dragon weren't sharing properly together and they were extremely naughty. Then they solved the problem because they took it in turns. They played dragons and horses and lastly unicorns. They had no arguments ever again.

Isabella Funnell (6)
Seaford Primary School, Seaford

Romeo's Space Story

One day, 500 years ago, a young man called Nik, was jogging with his friend Harry to a spaceship. 'Finally!' said Nik.
They got on the ship and lay down.
'Argh!' gasped Harry.
'Nice isn't it?' Nik said quietly.
'Wooo!'
'Let's go!'
'Let's go explore!' Nik bellowed. Just then, Nik bumped into two old friends.
'Tillos and Grog,' Nik screeched., 'what ya doing here?'
'Oh just popped by, bye!'
They walked 20 more miles, then... Harry touched the king of space's crown.
'Harry, no!' Nik screamed, but it was too late, a giant space monster came out from a rock! Nik hit it with his sword.
'Ha ya!' *Pow!* Harry shot it with his gun, *boom!*
When the monster was dead, Nik snatched its crown and became king of Earth and space.

Romeo Nitis (7)
Seaford Primary School, Seaford

Harry's Jungle Story

One gloomy night in a world far away there was a man called Tarzan, who had a friend called Gorilla.
One day an evil snake called Larry, created an army of evil snakes called Army of Snakes.
'Next week we will attack Tarzan,' said Larry, but Tarzan and Gorilla overheard Larry and were ready for the battle.
The day before the battle Tarzan swung from tree to tree and came to land and looked at Larry's base. They had army helmets and they were all fast asleep.
The next day it was battle day. Two hours later Tarzan and Gorilla won the battle.

Harry Martin (7)
Seaford Primary School, Seaford

Amelie's Space Story

Amy had a baby but Bob stole the baby and Amy needed to get the baby back. Amy got into the rocket and zoomed off to Mars to fight the alien and get the baby back to Earth.
It took a long time to get there but Amy finally got there.
Amy punched and kicked and hit the alien so he fell over onto the ground and hurt himself.
Amy grabbed the baby, jumped into the rocket and started the rocket right away.
In the morning the rocket landed on Earth.
Amy was very glad that the rocket had landed on Earth safely because Amy thought they were going to land with a bump.
Amy and the baby got a black taxi back to where Amy and the baby lived.

Amelie Fannon (7)
Seaford Primary School, Seaford

Simon's Magical Story

One Sunday afternoon there was a grown-up who had magical powers. She'd hid her powers for a long time because she accidentally hurt her sister, Anna.
One day a witch came along and took away Elsa's sister, Anna. The next day the witch came again and took away the king and queen so Elsa was all by herself with the family cat. She put up a picture so it would remind her of her family.
She got out a mirror and looked in it and instead of seeing herself, she saw her family in prison.
The next day the witch came to take Elsa away. Then Elsa saw her family in prison.
She thought she would be right next to them. The king broke free and said to the witch, 'You evil witch, you tricked Elsa, Anna, me and the queen,' and he defeated the witch.

Simon West (6)
Seaford Primary School, Seaford

Summer's Magical Story

My new house has a secret door and it leads to a witch's mansion and my friends, Josh and Ella go in it.
One day Josh and Ella went in it for a very long time, so I went in it of course. Do you know what I saw? A witch. She was trying to cook Ella and Josh. I tried to stop her but she got even worse.
She started to plan a spell to kill Josh and a spell to cook Ella. 'Ha ha ha!' she croaked but she saw me and I ran away and phoned the cops. She tried to turn me into dust and she said she was the last witch in the world. Then the cops arrested her and I put everything right again.

Summer Dann (6)
Seaford Primary School, Seaford

Lily-Anne's Magical Story

A long time ago there lived a princess called Ivy. She lived by herself. There was also an evil witch.
The witch was trying to catch Ivy but Ivy was very good because she ran into her house. One day the witch called her dragon out to catch her. He caught Ivy so she was locked up in the castle with tangled vines. They were very prickly and could spike you.
The witch came up in the castle and said, 'I will keep you here.'
Ivy used her long brush and then a handsome young prince came and they got married.

Lily-Anne Middleton (7)
Seaford Primary School, Seaford

Oliver's Space Story

Far, far away in space an alien called Blomxia was heading down to Earth.
When he got down there the people ran screaming into their houses.
Blomxia found the sea and then he wanted to rule the world so...
He threw someone into the sea head first!
But then someone threw Blomxia into the sea.
Everyone cheered as the queen threw the spaceship in the rubbish dump.

Oliver McFarlane (6)
Seaford Primary School, Seaford

Lara's Magical Story

Once upon a time in a beautiful castle lived a queen and king and they lived far, far away from the town.
One stormy morning a herd of magical planets came and tried to defeat the castle. They started a battle.
After the magical battle their house was a bit damaged so they moved house and the king and queen had a daughter.
As the princess got older she met her unicorn and they all lived together and had a disco party.

Lara Parekh (6)
Seaford Primary School, Seaford

Cerys' Under The Sea Story

There once lived a poor little boat called Garry, all Garry did was sail, sail and more sailing. Garry was always bored.
Then one day he began to sink. He was underwater and there, standing right in front of him, was a crab. 'Hello,' said the crab, 'what a nice day today.'
Suddenly a shark came. 'Help!' somebody shouted. At that very moment the shark gave a grin and swam off.
'Stop that shark!' a voice said.
The shark turned round and there was Ariel and her dad, King Triton.
'Go away!' shouted Garry.
'Hooray,' they all cheered, 'that boat saved me and my dad.'
'Thank you so much Garry,' they laughed, noticing the name label.
'Bye-bye Garry.'
'Creak, creak!' said Garry, that meant 'goodbye'.
Ariel said, 'Poor boat, we don't want to leave you so we will keep you.'

Cerys Hier (6)
Walberton & Binsted CE Primary School, Arundel

Charlotte's Dinosaur Story

One sunny day a mouse thought he would make a time machine. When it was built he tested it. Suddenly...
Unfortunately he landed in the land of the dinosaurs, there were two friendly dinosaurs, one was called Patty and one, Spike.
Just then they entered a rainforest. They went into some leaves, to the top of the forest and saw a T-rex.
The T-rex wanted the eggs of Mum Eller. He stomped and stomped, he nearly got the eggs but Mum Eller came to the rescue. She swooped silently down and got her three eggs.
The mouse found his little time machine and went home.

Charlotte Hughes (7)
Walberton & Binsted CE Primary School, Arundel

Erin's Under The Sea Story

One day there was a little boat, his name was Larry, but he had no owner so he had to find a new one. He decided to look underwater by swimming so fast.
He flipped over and this was no ordinary boat, it was a magical boat. He turned himself into the king of the sea. Suddenly a shark appeared from nowhere, he slashed his tail and gnashed his teeth.
Suddenly another book character appeared, it was Ariel and Larry who had turned himself into the sea king. He pointed his sceptre at the shark. 'Hooray!' shouted Ariel, the shark was so scared he ran away! Just then, along came Ariel's real father and Larry turned back into his real boat form. 'I am so happy you saved me, I will be your owner,' and they lived happily ever after.

Erin Mae Duff (6)
Walberton & Binsted CE Primary School, Arundel

Josie's Under The Sea Story

One sunny day, on the sea, there was nobody on the boat. There was nobody and it was quiet.
It was really noisy under the sea. Suddenly it was really windy and a current came.
A shark came because he smelt the mermaid and seahorse. The shark was called Tib.
The king mermaid was furious with the shark. He raised his fork and the shark swam away.
He was happy to see his daughter and she was happy to see her dad.
Luckily they saw the empty boat. They decided to climb in the boat and they sailed home.

Josie Van Deelen (7)
Walberton & Binsted CE Primary School, Arundel

Imogen's Jungle Story

One dark, rainy night a boy called Max, got lost in the forest. His mother said, 'If you get lost just retrace your steps.'
Then Max came across a kind little snake and he said, 'Are you lost? Then just retrace your steps.'
Then he came across a cobra, he put his hand on his heart and could feel it pumping fast. 'Argh!' and he ran away.
Then he saw a little lion, the lion said, 'Are you lost?'
'Yes,' said Max.
'I thought I heard your mother calling you.'
Then he started running. Max hurried behind him. 'Wait for me,' said Max.
He jumped on a log and said, 'Is this your home?'
'Yes,' said Max and he ran down the path to his house.

Imogen Grace Chapman (6)
Walberton & Binsted CE Primary School, Arundel

Annabelle's Magical Story

One hot morning a rainbow appeared next to a beautiful castle with three flags that were red, blue and green. There was a couple of trees.

Suddenly a dragon came along and hid behind a tree. Unfortunately the queen saw him but he thought that she couldn't but she could and the castle shook.

Just then there was a fire and the dragon thought he was going to win.

Suddenly, along came a magic unicorn that sorted the problem out.

They fell in love but the dragon was being cheeky and they had a fight.

After a while a wicked witch came. She tried to help the dragon kill the unicorn but she had a live broom.

He did not like the witch, it pointed to a cottage and the wicked witch got locked up in the cottage.

The unicorn and the dragon loved each other again then they all lived happily ever after.

Annabelle Knight (6)

Walberton & Binsted CE Primary School, Arundel

Aadam's Space Story

One strange evening there was a huge rocket from Earth. Suddenly there was a shooting star and it banged into the rocket and broke a leg.
The rocket landed on a strange planet but it was still next to Earth.
The astronaut was stuck on the strange planet.
Luckily a UFO came by and it was a friendly alien and it said it would help the astronaut get off the strange planet.
The alien was called Bob and it liked the astronaut.
Bob pressed a button, a beam from the bottom of the UFO lifted up the rocket.
The UFO took the rocket home and they lived happily ever after.

Aadam Gyening (7)
Walberton & Binsted CE Primary School, Arundel

David's Dinosaur Story

One sunny day there lived a boy called Bobby. One day he went shopping. He bought a machine, it was a time machine. He sat on it. Suddenly it took him to a dinosaur world. It was scary but he saw a dinosaur, it was friendly. The dinosaur's name was Sparky, it was a girl. Suddenly a fierce T-rex came. Sparky had some dinosaur eggs. The T-rex was hungry.
He crept up to the eggs, he was about to eat the eggs then Sparky came. She roared.
Her friend came and helped her. Her friend carried them away.
After a long time there Bobby went home and had supper, then it was bedtime.

David Harrison (7)
Walberton & Binsted CE Primary School, Arundel

Charlie's Magical Story

Once upon a time there was a huge castle and it had three blue flags.
Just then a dragon popped out of a bush, it looked scary but it was not...
Suddenly a different dragon jumped out. They had a battle.
The good dragon was called Berpee. After the fight Berpee went home.
Berpee asked the wizard if he could build the castle.
Fortunately the wizard said, 'Yes.'
'Abracadabra!' The castle was normal.

Charlie Matthews (7)
Walberton & Binsted CE Primary School, Arundel

Carla's Magical Story

One sunny morning there was a shiny, sparkly castle. Along came a dragon, he had flaming, fiery breath and sharp pointy teeth.
Along came a unicorn, she helped the dragon.
His burning breath came out. He was very angry and very, very scary.
Along came a friendly, glittery unicorn. She and the dragon shook hands. They were very, very happy.
Along came a scary wicked witch with a spot on her cheek and an alive broom.
The broom was pointing at a lovely little house near the bright moon.
The dragon and the unicorn went into the house.

Carla Tait-Bower (7)
Walberton & Binsted CE Primary School, Arundel

Finley's Dinosaur Story

One sunny day there lived a little boy called Bob. One day Bob went out and saw a time machine so he went on it.
It took him to the dinosaur times. The dinosaurs were very happy the way they lived.
Suddenly Sparky came over. He said, 'I want some dinner! Where is it?'
Then he saw some eggs. 'Yum-yum,' he said. He was just about to eat them until...
A pterodactyl swooped past Sparky and grabbed the eggs and gave the eggs back to Larry.
Then Bob went home and he said, 'Home sweet home.'

Finley Lennon Shackleton (7)
Walberton & Binsted CE Primary School, Arundel

Isaac's Space Story

One dark evening a man who always wanted to go to the white, light, cheese moon. He went up to space.
Suddenly he lost sight of the moon and found the Earth then he found the moon again and landed on the moon.
He found a spaceship that landed right next to him.
An alien said, 'Hello,' in a deep, dark voice. He said, 'Is your rocket broken?'
'Yes.'
'Do you need a lift?'
'Yes please.'
'First tell me where your house is.'
'It's in Walberton. It has a pond outside.'
'What's a pond?' and then he took me home.

Isaac Daniel (6)
Walberton & Binsted CE Primary School, Arundel

Phebe's Jungle Story

In a dark and spooky, rainy forest there lived a big green and yellow snake who was nice and happy slithering along the long smooth tree branch with lots of vines on it.
He felt so brave he decided to go further into the forest.
Suddenly he saw an enormous furry thing with big yellow eyes, big hairy paws and sharp claws.
Suddenly the lion jumped out of the leaves then went away but came back again.
So the snake followed the lion. He realised the lion was taking him home.
He was really pleased because he was really hungry.
So they went in their house and had something to eat.

Phebe Elderton (6)
Walberton & Binsted CE Primary School, Arundel

Eloïse's Dinosaur Story

One sunny day, there was a time machine in the garden. Outside there was a boy called Jon. Suddenly Jon saw the time machine in his garden. When his mum or dad were not looking, he tested it out and it worked! When he got out of the time machine, he saw a lot of dinosaurs and they were really kind and lovely but Jon saw a volcano.
Suddenly he saw a T-rex and his name was Sparky. He was so scared he even tried to hide somewhere but there was no hiding places so he had to stay still and be quiet so that's what he did.
Sparky wanted something to eat and he wanted to eat Edward's baby eggs. Sparky got closer and closer to the eggs. James the pterodactyl saw Sparky going to eat Edward's eggs.
James swooped down to the eggs but now Jon was not scared anymore. Jon saw the T-rex near the eggs and James swooping to the eggs in the sky.
Just in time the eggs were safe and then Jon had to go home in the time machine.

Eloïse Kirkton (6)
Walberton & Binsted CE Primary School, Arundel

Taylor's Space Story

One sunny day there was a red shiny rocket, a space man appeared, he saw the moon.
He crash-landed on the moon.
A flying saucer appeared and an alien jumped out.
The alien said, 'Do you need help?'
The spaceman replied, 'Yes.'
Then the alien carried the broken space rocket.
He dropped the space rocket. 'There we go,' said the alien.

Taylor Chittenden (7)

Walberton & Binsted CE Primary School, Arundel

Nathan's Dinosaur Story

One sunny day a boy called Natty went into his garden and found a time machine.
He was in prehistoric times.
He met a nice dinosaur called Pat and they walked until... They saw a big T-rex called Jaw, who was going to eat Pat's eggs.
Suddenly Natty swooped and grabbed the eggs. He safely landed on the ground and they played together for hours.
Then the time machine was beeping. He said bye-bye and went home.

Nathan Banfield (7)
Walberton & Binsted CE Primary School, Arundel

Freddie's Space Story

One sunny day a rocket took off to space, steaming with fire and smoke.
It flew around the whole entire world and it saw the beautiful view.
Suddenly the rocket saw a spaceship and the rocket crashed into the spaceship.
The alien laughed, 'Ha, ha, ha!' he went. The alien laughed even louder.
So the rocket got sucked and the spaceship flew off.
The rocket was flying and getting sucked into the spaceship.

Freddie Laurence (6)
Walberton & Binsted CE Primary School, Arundel

Farhan's Dinosaur Story

Once upon a time there was a boy called Sam. He sat on the car and
he went to the Land of Dinosaurs.
He saw dinosaurs eating grass.
There was a dinosaur who had sharp teeth.
Sam saw some eggs were hatching.
The dinosaur that was flying was a pterodactyl, it was not nice.
Sam eventually got home.

Farhan Khan
West Green Primary School, Crawley

Tyler's Dinosaur Story

Once upon a time there was a time machine that could go in the past, present and future.
In the picture there were dinosaurs and there was a volcano. It erupted! All the dinosaurs were scared and in the future was a boy called Baden and he was scared too.
There was a T-rex and Baden saw it, he was scared and he ran back to the baby dinosaur.
They were still in their eggs and Baden was saying, 'Oh no.' The T-rex was going to eat the eggs and he said, 'No you don't.'
Their mummy came and saw the T-rex and they fought and then they fell in love.
Baden ran back to the time machine to go back to his mum and he had dinner and the dinosaurs came with him.

Tyler Edwards (7)
West Green Primary School, Crawley

Duaa's Dinosaur Story

One day a little girl went on a time machine. She went to the past.
When she got there she found a dinosaur.
The dinosaur was scary looking, then she ran away.
She found a nice dinosaur, it was lovely.
There was a scary dinosaur, he was fierce.
The girl was scared. She ran away and she was safe.
The flying dinosaur laid three eggs, they were big and fat.
The flying dinosaur nearly died but he was safe.
She went home.

Duaa Kazmi (7)
West Green Primary School, Crawley

Zakariya's Dinosaur Story

Once upon a time a dinosaur sat on a time machine, then the dinosaur went back in time! The dinosaur saw his friend, T-rex.
Next the volcano was angry and it exploded, then the T-rex ran away.
The bad dinosaur came, then the good dinosaur. The bad dinosaur ran after him.
The good dinosaur saw some beautiful baby eggs.
A flying dragon came and took the baby eggs!
All of the dinosaurs went back to their own house.

Zakariya Azeem (6)
West Green Primary School, Crawley

Baden's Space Story

Once upon a time there lived a boy called Bob, he went to space.
When he reached the moon he put a flag on it.
Oh no, a flying saucer came! He was scared. The alien was inside the flying saucer and he laughed.
He kept on laughing and laughing.
The flying saucer picked up the spaceship.
The flying saucer went home.

Baden Hill-Anderson (7)
West Green Primary School, Crawley

Harsh's Dinosaur Story

Once upon a time there was a boy called Harsh and him and his friends were going to the past and they were going to the dinosaurs.
Finally they were in the past and Harsh was there and it was a lovely place.
There was an angry dinosaur and it tried to eat the boys, but it couldn't because they were running super fast!
The eggs were starting to hatch without their mummy and daddy and there were three dragons inside the eggs.
They were going to the little eggs and they were flying to them.
Then they finally got home quickly for dinner and dinner was delicious.

Harsh Bakhia (7)
West Green Primary School, Crawley

Tyreese's Under The Sea Story

Once upon a time there was a boat sailing under the sea. It was cloudy, there were a couple of birds.
There were fish, baby fish, crabs, sharks and weeds.
A scary shark came, he was naughty. No one liked him, everyone was terrified.
He wanted to gobble the mermaid up but when the shark took the mermaid she pulled herself and she got out. She said, 'I'm free, I'm never going near the shark again.' Everyone was happy.
The king said, 'You're never going near the shark again!'

Tyreese Stone (6)
West Green Primary School, Crawley

Justin's Space Story

There was once a rocket that flew into space and was aiming for the second man to go to the moon and represent it with a flag.
Unfortunately, the rocket crashed and he couldn't get back to Earth.
'Oh no!' said the astronaut.
Then a spaceship came. 'Yikes!' said the astronaut. It was speeding like the speed of light. It was supersonic! Then it crashed and an alien came out.
It was a friendly alien with three eyes. 'Phew!' said the astronaut.
'I see your rocket is damaged,' said the alien. 'I'll transport it to Earth.'
'Thank you,' said the astronaut. And so the alien did.
He may not have achieved it, but he was still safe, right in his own home.

Justin Pillas (7)
West Green Primary School, Crawley

Umar's Space Story

There was once a rocket that flew into space and was aiming to the moon, the astronauts hung on tight as they were going to crash.
Suddenly they arrived on the moon. They climbed out of the rocket and saw the world and stars.
Then a zooming, speedy UFO nearly crashed on the cold freezing moon, it was about to crash.
Out came an alien with googly eyes, it had three eyeballs and it had two teeth. The alien said, 'I will take you back to Earth.'
They said, 'Yes.'
The UFO took the rocket to Earth with the astronauts.
Finally they were on Earth and they lived happily ever after.

Umar Mohamed (6)
West Green Primary School, Crawley

Nicole's Magical Story

A long time ago, not so far away, there was a lovely castle full of magic. Nobody ever went there except the two guards, the king and a wizard who was locked in prison. One day they let the wizard out to see if he could do some proper magic.
A dragon came along and stamped his feet then he roared loudly! Everyone was scared, even the guards, the king and the wizard!
Once the dragon got there he breathed fire. It was light orange. The colour of him was red and he was called Bumpy. He was seven months old.
The dragon fell in love with a unicorn! It was amazing. The unicorn was called Cuddles. The colour of her was rainbow.
Along came a witch who had found an enchanted magical mop. Her name was Sammy. Her hair was green. Suddenly, the witch dropped the mop!
The enchanted mop ran home. Then the moon came out and she felt free, safe and happy. She never saw the witch again.

Nicole Cossey (7)
West Green Primary School, Crawley

Gracie's Magical Story

Once upon a time there was a princess locked in a tower all alone.
A dragon was guarding the castle so the princess didn't escape.
The dragon had dangerous fire to kill the princess!
The dragon and the princess unicorn fell in love!
The witch was going to curse the princess and the curse would kill her!
The witch made a paintbrush come alive.
The paintbrush escaped from the witch and found a house and
something terrible happened. The witch was there!

Gracie Legge (7)
West Green Primary School, Crawley

Alfie's Magical Story

A long time ago, not so far away there lived a castle full of magic, nobody went there except for the two guards, the king and the wizard.
A dragon came along and stamped his feet and roared. Everyone was scared, even the wizard, who was the loudest.
The dragon burnt the castle down, it was red and yellow. The dragon was called Bumpy, he was red and quiet.
The dragon fell in love, it was amazing, they kissed each other and they held hands and loved each other for ever and ever.
A magic paintbrush came to a witch and became the witch's friend and gave her some magic to make the paintbrush magic.
The paintbrush went back home and it was midnight.

Alfie John Torrington (7)
West Green Primary School, Crawley

Thomas' Magical Story

A long time ago, not so far away, there was a lovely castle full of magic. Nobody ever went there except the witch and a princess.
A dragon came along to the castle and it was big and spiky.
Once the dragon got there it breathed light orange fire. It burned the castle.
Down in the garden a unicorn and a dragon fell in love.
The witch enchanted a paintbrush.
The paintbrush went up a hill and the witch was there.

Thomas Brown (7)
West Green Primary School, Crawley

Jessica's Magical Story

Once upon a time there was a princess in the tall castle alone and she was singing, she had a lovely voice.
Then the dragon came to see the princess, the dragon thought she had a lovely voice.
The dragon blew fire out of his mouth, it was boiling. It was brand new, the fire.
Then he saw a unicorn and they kissed on the lips. The unicorn was magic, so the unicorn knew that he was magic. She bit the dragon!
Then the dragon was dead.
The witch put a spell on the princess' dad and mum to make them fall asleep. The witch told the princess and she cried all night.
The wand was laughing that the princess' mum and dad were asleep.

Jessica Geoghegan (6)
West Green Primary School, Crawley

Sam's Magical Story

A princess was locked in a tower all alone.
A dragon was guarding the castle so the princess didn't escape.
The dragon had dangerous fire to kill the princess.
The dragon and the princess' unicorn fell in love!
The witch was going to curse the princess and the curse was to kill her! The witch enchanted a paintbrush.
The paintbrush found a house and something happened, the witch was there...

Sam Barker (6)
West Green Primary School, Crawley

Lacey's Magical Story

Once upon a time there was a magical castle with a beautiful rainbow.
A pretty princess went out to see the rainbow.
A dragon saw the princess and started sneaking up on her.
The princess noticed the dragon started breathing fire. The princess ran but the dragon was so fast that he caught her!
A unicorn looked at the dragon and the dragon dropped the princess.
A witch was nearby and she cast a spell on her broom that made it come alive!
She sent the broom to a little house and in the house there was another witch!

Lacey (6)
Wylye Valley CE (VA) Primary School, Warminster

Hector's Dinosaur Story

Jack was going to his dad's workshop and he found a machine and he ended up on a planet.
On the planet there were dinosaurs and the boy saw the dinosaurs.
'Is that a meat eater? Is it going to eat me?' he said.
'Where is the owner of the nest?'
A dinosaur was flying over the eggs.
He was scared when he got home and his mum and dad weren't there.

Hector McGregor (5)
Wylye Valley CE (VA) Primary School, Warminster

Emily's Magical Story

Once upon a time there was a beautiful castle on the hill and a rainbow over the castle. A princess was at the door which was blue. Her name was Rose. There was going to be a ball.

Suddenly a dragon came to the castle! He wanted the princess so he could eat her. She said, 'No!'

Then the dragon breathed fire and more fire! He wanted that princess so badly, he blew the castle down. Then he was gone!

The dragon saw a unicorn. He scratched the unicorn. She had a scratch that was bleeding really badly.

The witch came along. The witch had a talking broom. Suddenly, she got on her broom and raced to the princess at the castle.

There the broom went to a house that didn't look like the princess' castle at all.

Emily Jane Sweeting (5)

Wylye Valley CE (VA) Primary School, Warminster

Adlay's Jungle Story

Once upon a time there was a little boy called Jake. He went to the forest for a walk. Suddenly, a bunch of the eyes looked at him!
They looked cross then he saw a snake! It slithered towards him! Jake was scared and Jake ran away!
The snake slithered up Jake. He tried and he was pushing it away and then a lion came to help him. It fought with the snake but it was a friendly lion.
Then they played hide-and-seek. The lion won five times. Next they played it. It was very funny.
He saw that the lion was very fast. It was a talking lion! Jake the lion said, 'Come and see my house.' He let Jake in for tea.
His house was very nice. He had a big yard to play in. They had great fun.

Adlay Nicholas Nielsen-Hunt (6)
Wylye Valley CE (VA) Primary School, Warminster

Sophia's Magical Story

Once upon a time there was a lovely castle on a hill. It was a beautiful day so a girl went outside to see the rainbow.
One day a dragon saw the castle and breathed a fire on the castle.
The dragon breathed fire again. He roared and he roared and roared again and flew away.
The dragon landed in a field. A pony saw the dragon and they became friends.
One day a witch had a talking broom. The broom smiled and whooshed away. The broom zoomed around.
The broom saw a little house and flew to it. When the broom got to the house he cast a spell.

Sophia Mae Passmore (5)
Wylye Valley CE (VA) Primary School, Warminster

Espen's Dinosaur Story

Thomas was in a chair, the clock went to half-past six and Thomas was in Dinosaur Land.
He was scared in Dinosaur Land because there were too many dinosaurs. Then he saw a stegosaurus. He thought to himself and said, 'I like this land...'
'Uh-oh! There's a T-rex, he's going to eat me! I'd better run away.'
The T-rex saw him and chased him.
He climbed a tree. Suddenly he saw three eggs on the tree and he said, 'Who could these belong to?'
Next he saw a flying dinosaur. 'Oh, they are his eggs on this tree.' The dinosaur waved at Thomas and Thomas waved at him.
Thomas arrived safely back at home. His mum said, 'Where have you been, Thomas?'
'I went to Dinosaur Land.'
His mum said, 'Wow!'

Espen Longlands (5)
Wylye Valley CE (VA) Primary School, Warminster

Kathleen's Under The Sea Story

Once upon a time there was a boy called Tom. He rode a boat but then rain clouds came and the boat filled up with water.
He fell in. A mermaid came and saved Tom.
There was a shark, he was looking for food. He saw Tom and wanted to eat him up.
The mermaid was brave and got her dad. They scared the shark away.
They all started dancing and everyone was happy.
The mermaid put Tom back in his boat and they all lived happily ever after.

Kathleen Moore (4)
Wylye Valley CE (VA) Primary School, Warminster

Molly's Under The Sea Story

Once upon a time there was a king in the sea with a little girl and Tom saw the little girl and fell in love.
Suddenly Tom turned into a merman and then a crab turned up and he found the little girl.
The shark saw them and wanted to eat them up for his dinner.
The mermaid came and got her dad because he had a spear to push him away.
Everyone was happy and so they had a party.
At the end they went back to the boat and they all lived happily ever after.

Molly Temperance Carpenter (4)
Wylye Valley CE (VA) Primary School, Warminster

Charlotte's Magical Story

The palace is beautiful and pink. There are three beautiful and pink flags. There is a beautiful rainbow.
Then a fierce, bad, green dragon flies high.
The dragon blows fire and he blows and he blows and the castle falls down.
Luckily the queen was OK. Then a unicorn comes, it has a very pointy horn.
A witch comes and she has a magic spoon.
The spoon sees a house. The house is empty so he lives there for ever.

Charlotte Tory (5)
Wylye Valley CE (VA) Primary School, Warminster

THE END!

YOUNG WRITERS INFORMATION

We hope you have enjoyed reading this book - and that you will continue to enjoy it in the coming years.

If you like reading and creative writing drop us a line, or give us a call, and we'll send you a free information pack.

Alternatively if you would like to order further copies of this book or any of our other titles, then please give us a call or log onto our website at www.youngwriters.co.uk.

Young Writers Information
Remus House
Coltsfoot Drive
Peterborough
PE2 9BF
(01733) 890066